¡Am Famous!

Hey, peoples!

It's me, Carly! And you brilliant fans know by now that this is the latest installment in the chronicles of *iCarly*. Thanks to you, the Web show is reaching more viewers than ever! We've even gotten the attention of some big-time shoe company and television executives. Can you believe it?

These dudes had lots of ideas for changing *iCarly*. Change can be good. (Have you tried night breakfast? I highly recommend you give Canadian bacon a try. Yum, eh?) But some changes can lead to a giant exploding mess! It's a good thing Spencer is so creative, Freddie knows his way around all the tech stuff, and Sam is always hungry to solve a problem. . . . Okay, who am I kidding? The only problem Sam's eager to solve is where to get more salami and pudding.

But anyway, want to know about the totally ridiculous people that tried to take over *iCarly*? It's all right here. Just sit back and kick off your shoes . . . and hope they don't burst into flames. That reminds me — don't forget to take a look at the insane photos, too. What are you waiting for?! Turn the page! ☺

And don't forget to keep watching *iCarly*. Bye!

People of Earth — don't miss a single
iCarly book!

¡Am Famous!

Adapted by Laurie McElroy

**Part 1: Based on the episode "iPromote Tech-Foots"
Written by Arthur Gradstein**

**Part 2: "iCarly Saves Television"
Written by Jake Farrow**

**Based on the TV series *iCarly*
Created by Dan Schneider**

SCHOLASTIC INC.

New York   Toronto   London   Auckland   Sydney
Mexico City   New Delhi   Hong Kong   Buenos Aires

No part of this work may be reproduced, stored in a retrieval system, or transmitted in any form or by any means, electronic, mechanical, photocopying, recording, or otherwise, without written permission of the publisher. For information regarding permission, write to Scholastic Inc., Attention: Permissions Department, 557 Broadway, New York, NY 10012.

ISBN–13: 978-0-545-15525-0
ISBN–10: 0-545-15525-8

Published by Scholastic Inc.
SCHOLASTIC and associated logos are trademarks and/or registered trademarks of Scholastic Inc.

12 11 10 9 8 7 6 5 4 3   9 10 11 12 13 14/0

Printed in the U.S.A.
First printing, September 2009

iPromote Tech-Foots

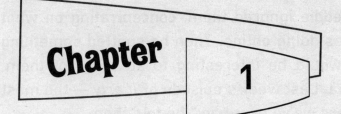

Chapter 1

Carly Shay and her best friend, Sam Puckett, were kicking back on Carly's couch after school, watching television. Carly's friend and neighbor Freddie Benson sat in a chair nearby, surfing the Web on his laptop.

Sam groaned. "I am *soooo* hungry," she said.

Carly wasn't surprised. Sam was always hungry. She usually made herself at home in Carly's kitchen, poking around in the refrigerator and the pantry as if they were her own. "So go make something," Carly told her.

Sam groaned again and dropped her head on Carly's shoulder. "I am *soooo* lazy," she said.

Carly laughed and shook her head. She knew Sam wanted her to get up and make her something to eat, but Sam could make her own snack.

Freddie ignored them, concentrating on what he was doing online. Then he spotted something that would be interesting to all three of them. "Whoa. Last week's episode of *iCarly* — the most viewers we've ever had," he told them.

iCarly was a weekly live Webcast that Carly worked on with her friends. Carly had gotten the idea for the show when a teacher at their school had turned away the most interesting acts for the school's talent show. Carly decided to give her friends an online showcase for their weird and wacky talents. Her show became the only place to catch the eighth grader who could repeat sentences backwards, the girl who hopped on a pogo stick while she played the trumpet, and the boy who would eat absolutely anything.

Freddie was the show's technical producer. Not only did he have all the latest camera equipment and other high-tech gadgets, he knew how to use them. He was always coming up with new ways to make their live weekly Webcast and their Website more exciting. Even the name *iCarly* had been Freddie's idea. "I — Internet. Carly — you," he had explained at the time.

Carly and Sam both loved the name. Ever since then, they'd appeared live on their fans' computer screens every single week in the show they called *iCarly*.

Sam was just as important to *iCarly*'s success as Carly and Freddie were. She was Carly's funny sidekick on the show and in real life. In addition to being a great friend, Sam was crazy, fun, and unpredictable. She was hilarious on and off the Webcast. No one was as good as Sam at coming up with wild ideas — especially ones designed to torture Freddie.

To say the two of them got on each other's nerves was a major understatement. Carly often found herself playing peacemaker between them. But they all agreed on one thing: making the show was totally fun.

So far the weekly Webcast had been a hit. More kids were tuning in every week and telling their friends to watch, too. And now Freddie had discovered that they had just had their biggest audience ever.

"Really?" Carly asked, running her hand through her long, dark hair.

Sam sat up, her hunger forgotten. "How many?"

"Three hundred fifty-five thousand," Freddie said happily.

Carly jumped to her feet. "Whoa!" she said, completely blown away. That was an impressive number.

"Awesome!" Sam added, giving both of her friends a high five.

They were still amazed at their huge audience when Carly's brother, Spencer, burst into the apartment looking frazzled. He slammed the door behind him.

Spencer was Carly's guardian while their father, a military officer, was stationed overseas. It wasn't typical for a thirteen-year-old girl to live with her twenty-six-year-old brother, but Carly and Spencer wouldn't have it any other way.

Spencer was an artist. Carly always said that part of the fun of living with him was never knowing what new piece of art she would find at home — a giant robot sculpture made out of soda bottles, a fish-feeding machine, or a camcorder transformed into a squirrel. Spencer was definitely quirky and offbeat, but he was always there for his little sister. He was totally responsible when it came to the important stuff like making sure Carly ate healthy foods and did well in school, and Carly helped Spencer tone down some of his wildest art ideas. The two of them looked out for each other.

Spencer had been cool with the idea of Carly and her friends turning the third floor of their loft in downtown Seattle into a studio for the Webcast. It was a big open space, and they had fixed it up to look amazing. There was plenty of room for all of Freddie's high-tech equipment, and Spencer's sculptures made awesome props. His sculpture of the front end of a classic car was in the background of every show, along with a wall painted with the moon and stars. There was even a neon *iCarly* Live sign over the window.

Carly checked her watch. It was pretty late. Spencer was usually home when she got back from school. "Hey, where've you been all day?" she asked.

"Canada," Spencer said, obviously upset.

"Canada?" Sam asked.

7

Carly was confused, too. "I thought you were just going to the art museum," she said.

"I was. Until I fell asleep on the bus and woke up in Vancouver," Spencer explained. "I am so done with public transportation."

"Ah, it's not that bad," Sam told him. "You know, I was born on a bus."

Born on a bus? Everyone gave Sam a curious look.

"My mom's not good at planning," she said defensively.

Carly let it drop and turned back to her brother. "I'm not sure it's fair to blame the bus because you fell asleep," she told him.

"Not just that. Last week on the bus someone spilled chili on me," Spencer said with a shudder. "Then continued to eat it. Without a spoon."

Carly laughed. "I can't believe you went all the way to Canada."

Spencer walked into the kitchen. "It wasn't a total loss. I bought Canadian bacon while I was there." He held up a brown paper bag that read *Bacon, eh?* "Who wants night breakfast?" he asked.

8

"Meeee!" Carly, Sam, and Freddie said together.

Carly's cell phone chimed. The people who usually called or texted her were already in the room.

"Text message?" Freddie asked.

Carly pulled her phone out of her pocket and then shook her head. "Email," she said, clicking the screen. "From the president of Daka," she added, totally confused.

"Daka the shoe company?" Sam asked.

Carly nodded. "Yeah."

"Read it," Sam said impatiently.

"'Dear Carly: We're big fans of your Web show,'" Carly read.

"Wow," Sam said, looking over Carly's shoulder.

Freddie couldn't believe employees at a big company like Daka were actually watching *iCarly*. "Cool," he said.

Carly kept reading, her voice rising with excitement. "'We'd love to have a meeting with you in our Seattle office and talk about a business relationship between Daka Shoes and *iCarly*.'"

Sam's jaw dropped. "No way," she said.

Freddie grinned. "That's awesome."

They heard a groan from the kitchen. Spencer had opened his Canadian bacon. He held a slice between his fingers and waved it at them. "This stuff is just sliced ham!" he yelled. "How dare those Canadians try to pass this off as some sort of fancy bacon!" He gave the bacon a sniff, and then took a bite and started to chew.

Carly, Sam, and Freddie just watched him, speechless. Was Spencer actually upset because his bacon was too much like ham?

Obviously, Spencer's disappointment was short-lived. He grabbed another slice. Canadian bacon might be just ham, but it was really *good* ham.

Chapter 2

The next day after school, Carly, Sam, and Freddie headed to Daka's downtown office for a meeting. A woman named Sandra gave them a quick tour of the offices and then led them through a set of glass doors.

"And this is our conference room," she said.

"Cool," Carly said, looking around the room. Each chair around the huge conference table had a different sneaker mounted on top as a headrest. There were also shoes on display everywhere along with Daka advertising posters. Each seat at the table had a pad and pencil in front of it. It all looked very official and businesslike . . . and more than a little intimidating.

"Nice," Freddie said.

Sam took a bite of a turkey sandwich and looked around. "I like it," she added.

"Where'd you get the sandwich?" Carly asked.

Sam shrugged. "Found it on some dude's desk," she answered.

Carly shook her head. The world should know by now: Unattended food in Sam's vicinity tended to get eaten — fast.

Sandra gave Sam a strange look. "Uh, have a seat," she said. "Our executive team will be in shortly."

The kids sat at the table.

"All right, let's go over the game plan," Carly said, as soon as Sandra left the room.

"What do you mean?" Sam asked.

Freddie didn't understand either. They didn't know what the game was yet — how could they have a plan? "We don't even know what they want from us," he said.

Carly had been thinking about it. She had an idea as to why Daka wanted this meeting. "Well, they probably know that lots of people watch *iCarly*, so I bet they want us to promote some shoes or something."

"Cool," Sam said.

"Yeah, if they pay us," Freddie agreed. "We should get fifty bucks cash or no deal."

"Fifty?" Sam said. "*iCarly*'s got a huge audience. We should get at least a hundred."

Carly thought about that for a minute. "Okay. We'll ask for a hundred." Then she started to worry. Was that too much to ask for? Would the Daka people get mad and change their minds? "I hope they don't think that's pushy," she said nervously.

Sam didn't worry about being too aggressive. No one would ever accuse her of being a pushover. "Yeah, I'd hate for anyone to think *I'm* pushy," she said sarcastically.

A couple of guys in suits came into the conference room. "I swear," one of them said to the other. "One minute my turkey sandwich was sitting there on my desk, and then . . . gone."

"Get over it, Braxley," the second man told him.

Braxley shook his head. "I'm clueless. . . ." he said.

The *iCarly* team stood. The second man shook their hands enthusiastically. He knew them all by name. "Carly, Sam, Freddie," he said. "I'm Greg Horvath, president of Daka Shoes."

The president! Carly couldn't believe that the company's president was meeting with them. The one hundred dollars was looking more and more likely.

"Please, sit down. Have a seat," Mr. Horvath said. "We have a lot to discuss."

More executives streamed into the room behind him and took their seats around the table.

"Our marketing team is very familiar with your Web show, *iCarly*," Mr. Horvath said.

"Yes," Braxley added.

"We are," said a woman at the end of the table.

The rest of the executives nodded in agreement.

"Apparently, you're getting three hundred thousand viewers a week," Mr. Horvath said.

"More," Freddie said proudly.

Mr. Horvath nodded. "Impressive. And that's why Daka would like to advertise our new sneaker on your show."

Carly, Sam, and Freddie all exchanged knowing looks. Carly decided she could *definitely* ask for one hundred dollars and hold firm.

Sandra carried a round metal container with

the Daka logo into the room. There was steam coming out of the top of it, as if something inside was smoking hot.

"Here it is!" someone whispered.

The executives all buzzed with excitement.

The excitement was contagious. The *iCarly* team leaned forward, eager to see what all the buzz was about.

Mr. Horvath pressed a button and talked into a microphone on the table. His deep voice was amplified throughout the room. "Daka's new . . ." he paused and removed the lid of the container with a dramatic flourish. Inside was a single sneaker. ". . . Tech-Foot," he said.

The sneaker turned on a pedestal giving everyone in the room a complete view. Lights in the heel flashed as it revolved.

The executives applauded.

"Awesome!" Freddie said, standing to give it a closer look.

"Sweet shoe," Sam added.

Carly didn't know what all the fancy buttons were for, but she knew trendy when she saw it. "That's so cool!"

"The Tech-Foot is our most technologically-advanced shoe ever," Mr. Horvath explained. "It has a pedometer, so you know exactly how many steps you've run, walked, or jogged. It has a foot warmer for when your feet get cold. And it even offers Wi-Fi connectivity."

Braxley grinned. "I call it Shoe-Fi," he said.

Mr. Horvath didn't like being interrupted, and he didn't think Braxley's joke was clever at all. "Braxley!" he scolded.

"I'm clueless. . . ." Braxley said, slinking down into his seat.

Carly wondered exactly how Mr. Horvath wanted to advertise the shoe on *iCarly*. It wasn't like they ran commercials on the Webcast or anything like that. "So, how do you want us to —"

Mr. Horvath expected Carly's question and cut her off with a wave of his hand. He wouldn't tell her. Instead, he would show Carly exactly what he wanted her and Sam to do. "Lights!" he ordered.

One of the executives jumped up and turned off the lights.

"Screen!" Mr. Horvath commanded.

Another executive aimed a remote control at a plasma screen TV and pressed a button. A picture of Carly and Sam appeared on the screen. They were each holding a Tech-Foot sneaker. The next thing Carly and Sam knew, the mouths in the picture were moving, but it wasn't their voices coming out of them. Daka had used pictures of Carly and Sam, and recorded other voices to speak for them.

"I'm Carly," the picture of Carly said.

"I'm Sam," said Sam's picture.

"We love the new Tech-Foot," the picture of Carly said.

Her on-screen sidekick answered. "Yes, the new Tech-Foot."

"They're fantastic," the pictures said together.

The real Carly and Sam eyed each other. It was totally weird hearing those random voices coming out of their own mouths.

Mr. Horvath signaled his executives. They turned off the TV and turned on the lights.

"That's what we want you to do," he explained to the *iCarly* team.

Freddie couldn't believe how easy that would

be. "Carly and Sam just talk about the shoes while they're doing *iCarly*?"

"Exactly," Mr. Horvath answered. "Because if your audience knows that you guys love the new Tech-Foot, then they'll go out and buy them."

Sam was tired of all the speeches. It was time to get to business. "So, how much are you gonna pay us?" she demanded.

Carly flinched. "Sam, you don't say it like that," she whispered. She turned to Mr. Horvath and smiled. "So, how much are you going to pay us?" she asked sweetly.

"How much do you want?" Mr. Horvath asked.

Carly exchanged looks with Sam and Freddie. They both nodded slightly, letting her know she should ask for one hundred dollars.

"We want a hundred," Carly said. Then she sank down in her seat, sure that Mr. Horvath would laugh at them for asking for so much.

Freddie held his breath.

Sam was much more relaxed. She took a bite of her stolen sandwich while Mr. Horvath signaled the others in the room. There were nods around the table.

"Deal," Mr. Horvath said. "We'll pay you one hundred thousand dollars."

One hundred *thousand* dollars? That was a thousand times more money than they thought they could get!

Sam choked on her turkey sandwich. Carly and Freddie slapped her on the back. The chunk in Sam's throat flew across the table. And it landed in front of Braxley! He narrowed his eyes and picked it up, examining the bread and the fillings. He recognized the Muenster cheese. That was his sandwich! He was ready to confront the sandwich thief when Mr. Horvath cut him off.

"Braxley!" he said, in a warning tone of voice.

Braxley got rid of the evidence by popping it into his mouth and chewing.

Even Sam thought that was gross.

Mr. Horvath turned to the *iCarly* team. "Now, one hundred thousand dollars paid over one year comes to . . ."

"More than eight thousand dollars a month," Braxley said, clearly pleased with his ability to do the math so quickly in his head.

Mr. Horvath gave him a disgusted frown, then turned back to the kids. "Do we have a deal?" he asked.

Carly pretended to think about it for one second. "Ummm . . . yes," she said with an excited smile.

"Uh-huh," Sam said, still a little stunned.

"Yeah," Freddie added, nodding his head happily.

"Excellent," Mr. Horvath told them. He signaled one of his employees. Three contracts and three pens were placed in front of the *iCarly* team. "Just sign these contracts, and you'll get your first check."

Check?

"Whoa, wait, whoa, whoa," Sam said. "We want cash."

Carly and Freddie nodded in agreement.

The executives paused for a moment, staring at Mr. Horvath for guidance. He nodded, and they all pulled out their wallets and started handing over cash.

"Keep it coming," Sam said, taking a twenty. "Yep, keep it coming."

Freddie's eyes lit up as more money than he had ever seen before was handed to him. He admired the picture of Ben Franklin on a one hundred dollar bill. "This is good," he said.

Carly grinned. "This is fun," she said. "This is a fun time."

The cash piled up in front of them, and all they had to do in exchange was say nice things about the coolest shoe ever. How easy was that?

Chapter 3

A few days later, Carly was heading home after her latest shopping spree. Finding ways to spend her Tech-Foot money was the most fun ever. She bounced down the hall wearing a cool new pair of sunglasses, carrying tons of shopping bags, and singing a song as she went. "And I bought some stuff because I know I got paid the other day," she sang.

She stopped to pound on Freddie's door. "Freddie, come over!" she yelled, and then unlocked the door to her own apartment, resuming her song. "I'm having fun with Daka's money. I'm spending a ton of Daka's money. I'm a rich girl!"

She had just set down her bags on the kitchen counter, still humming, when Freddie walked in. "Looking good, Carly," Freddie said, admiring her new shades.

"Feeling good, Freddie," Carly said. "So what did you buy?" she asked.

"Oh, just this," Freddie answered, holding up a new DiVaglio laptop computer.

"New laptop?" Carly asked.

Freddie chuckled. "This isn't just a laptop," he told her. "This is the DiVaglio — the finest, best, most insanely awesome portable computer known to man. Listen to the sound it makes when you open it." Freddie opened the laptop and it was like a choir of angels was singing. Freddie practically wiggled with happiness. He closed the laptop again with a satisfied smile.

"Sweet," Carly said.

"So what'd you buy?" Freddie asked, noticing all the shopping bags.

"Some awesome sunglasses from . . ." Carly held up a bag. "Mercedes Lens!"

"Hoo-hoo! Fancy," Freddie laughed.

"Okay, tell me which pair you like better!" Carly put on a pair of oval frames with dark lenses. "These?" she asked, striking a pose. "Or these?" she said, changing to a pair of square frames.

Freddie was kind of hopeless when it came to

fashion. Plus he liked Carly in everything she wore. "Uhhhh," he mumbled.

But Carly wasn't finished. She slipped on some round frames. "Or these?" she asked. Then she pulled out another oval pair, but this pair had blue lenses. "These are interesting."

"How many did you buy?" Freddie asked.

Carly was giddy with the excitement of spending all that money. "I stopped counting after thirty!" she told him.

Freddie was giddy too. Having money was the coolest. "Side five!" he said.

He and Carly slapped their palms together and then the back of their hands.

They were still reveling in their riches when they heard a bell. Spencer wheeled an extremely odd-looking contraption into the room. Carly could tell that it was a bicycle, but how many bikes had Spencer used to put it together? The front and back wheels were different sizes. The handlebars looked more like a mini football goalpost, and the seat looked like a baby seat that was supposed to go behind the bike's main seat. A pair of fuzzy dice hung from the handlebars, and what looked like a radio antenna was attached to the back of the seat. It was the kind of bike that only Spencer could make.

Spencer spotted Carly's shopping bags. "Oooh, you guys having some fun spending your Daka money?" he asked.

"Oh yeah," Carly said.

"Yeah, we are," Freddie added.

"What is that?" Carly asked.

"Oh. Well, since I refuse to ride the bus anymore, I made myself this bike out of parts I found at the junkyard," Spencer explained.

Freddie was confused. "What's wrong with the bike you already have?" he asked.

"I don't have a bike," Spencer answered.

Carly laughed. "Yeah you do. It's hanging in the kitchen right there." She pointed to the bicycle that hung from the kitchen ceiling. Carly always wondered what would happen if somebody really tall came over. He or she would have to duck every time they wanted a drink of water.

Spencer stared at the bike on the ceiling openmouthed. It had been hanging there for such a long time that he had completely forgot that he even had a bike. He gave Carly and Freddie a shrug. He kind of liked his new homemade bike. "Well, too late now," he said, heading toward the front door.

Sam walked in as he was leaving. A woman in a blue coat trailed behind her.

"What-up?" Sam asked Spencer.

"Built a bike. Later," Spencer told her.

"Later," Sam said.

The woman with Sam closed the door behind Spencer, and the two of them walked into the apartment.

Sam ran over to her friends. The woman stayed right on her heels. "Hey, did Daka deliver the Tech-Foots yet?" she asked.

"Yeah, they're up in the studio," Carly told her.

"Nice," Sam said, flopping down on the couch and picking up a magazine.

The woman in the blue coat stood by, smiling.

Carly looked from Sam to the mystery woman and back to Sam again waiting for an explanation.

"Oh, sorry," Sam said. "Carly, Freddie, this is Sonya, my personal chef."

Sonya smiled and waved happily. "Yoo-hoo," she said with a thick accent.

"What?' "Carly asked.

"You hired a personal chef?" Freddie asked, just as shocked.

"Well, since I've got some real money now, why not?" she said with a shrug. She turned to the chef. "Sonya, please make me a grilled cheese sandwich with tomato."

Sonya nodded happily. "Yes, Miss Sam," she said, heading for the kitchen.

Suddenly, Carly was seeing the beauty of this arrangement. "I like grilled cheese sandwiches with tomato," she said, hinting.

Sam called out to Sonya. "Make that two, please."

"Yes, Miss Sam," Sonya said.

Freddie wanted in on the meal, too. "I like grilled cheese sandwiches with tomato."

Sam eyed him. "Tough nubs," she said.

Freddie glared back at her. He should have known that was coming.

Half an hour later, Carly and Freddie were upstairs in the studio trying on their new

27

Tech-Foots. Sam had already put hers on. She leaned back in a beanbag chair, finishing her second sandwich. Sonya waited nearby, ready to follow whatever orders Sam gave her.

"*Mmmmm*," Sam said, swallowing the last bite. "Sonya!"

Sonya hurried over.

"I'm done with this plate," Sam told her.

Sonya took the plate. "Dessert?" she asked.

Sam put her hand on her stomach. "I really shouldn't," she protested.

"I can make you cake," Sonya told her.

It didn't take much to turn Sam's no into a yes. "I'm thinking pie," she said.

"I will make pie." Sonya scurried off to the kitchen.

Carly finished tying her shoes and stood up. "Maybe it's just me, but didn't the Tech-Foot shoe they showed us at Daka look better than these?" she asked.

Freddie looked down at his shoes. They didn't seem to have as many cool features as the shoe in the conference room. "Yeah, I think you're right," he said.

28

"Who cares?" Sam asked. "I've got a lady making me pie." She stood up to join Carly and Freddie as they walked around in their new shoes. They all heard a loud chirping sound.

"They're kind of squeaky," Freddie said.

"Yeah, they're just new. Probably need to be broken in a little bit," Carly told him.

"Right," Freddie said.

Sam nodded. "True."

Freddie picked up his camera. "Okay, *iCarly* goes live in fifteen seconds."

"Let's shake it, baby," Sam said.

Carly and Sam jumped up and down to raise their energy levels while Freddie clicked some buttons on his computer control panel. The girls heard lots more squeaking from their shoes, but ignored it. They had a show to do.

Freddie walked toward them with his camera and began the countdown. "In five, four, three, two . . ." Instead of saying the number one, he pointed at the girls — their cue to begin the show.

"*Helloooooooo*, people," they said into the camera.

"You're watching *iCarly*," Carly told their viewers.

"I'm Sam," Sam said.

"So I must be Carly," Carly added.

Sam turned to her friend. "So Carly . . ."

"So Sam . . ." Carly answered.

"Why don't we tell everybody about the insanely awesome new shoes we got the other day?" Sam suggested.

"You know, we should," Carly said to Sam. Then she turned back to the camera. "Okay, these bad boys are called Tech-Foots."

Sam made a whooshing noise. It sort of sounded like the Daka company's logo. "By Daka," she said.

Carly and Sam plopped down onto two bean-bag chairs and waved their feet at the camera to show off their shoes.

As usual, the girls finished each other's sentences, cutting back and forth to keep up the kind of funny *iCarly* banter that their fans expected.

"And not only do they look cool," Carly began.

"They also have a built-in foot warmer," Sam added.

Carly continued to list the Tech-Foot's cool features. "They have a digital pedometer to tell you how far you've run, walked, or jogged . . ."

"They even have Wi-Fi connectivity!" Sam said. "Who wouldn't want these shoes?"

Carly raised her arms up in the air in an "I don't know" gesture as if she couldn't imagine anyone.

"Yeah, so go buy yourself a pair of Tech-Foots!" Sam yelled into the camera.

Together, Carly and Sam made the whooshing noise. "By Daka," they said smiling.

Okay! They had done their duty to Daka and earned their one hundred thousand dollars. The rest of that week's *iCarly* was their usual mix of jokes, comedy routines, and videos sent in by viewers. They tried to ignore the squeaking, but the noise was even louder than when Carly and Sam had hatched baby chicks for their science project. Throughout the entire show, Carly, Sam, and Freddie filled the studio with chirping sounds every time they took a step.

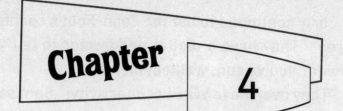

Chapter 4

A couple of days later in school, Sam limped down the stairs, squeaking with each step. The noises hadn't stopped as the shoes were broken in. In fact, they had gotten even worse.

Sam sat on a bench and pulled her sneaker off to rub her foot. Freddie spotted her and squeaked his way across the hall.

"Hey. Your feet hurt, too?" Freddie asked.

"Yeah, these Tech-Foots are killing me," Sam said.

"Mine, too," Freddie told her. But that wasn't all. "Oh, and last night? I tried to use the Wi-Fi on them and they crashed my new DiVaglio." He walked in a small circle listening to the sound his shoes made. "And I think these things are squeaking even louder."

"I know!" Sam said. "Mine are, too."

It was pretty rare for the two of them to agree on something, but they both had to admit that the Tech-Foots were not anywhere near as cool as Daka claimed them to be. The whole deal with Daka was starting to feel like a bad idea.

They walked around in little circles together, listening to their shoes squeak. They were *definitely* louder.

Carly walked up to them in her socks, carrying her Tech-Foots. Not only did she look stunned and scared, her hair stood out in a huge poof around her face like she had just stuck her finger into an electric socket!

"Oh my gosh!" Sam said.

Freddie's jaw dropped. "What happened?"

"I stepped in a little puddle and my Tech-Foots shocked me!" she said, holding up her sneakers. They were completely destroyed.

"Really?!" Sam asked.

"No way!" Freddie exclaimed.

"And then they totally fell apart!" Carly yelled.

Suddenly, the hall was filled with that familiar chirping sound, but Sam and Freddie were both standing still, and Carly wasn't even wearing her shoes. They looked around for the source and watched in horror as an angry mob of their class-mates walked up to them. They were all wearing Tech-Foots, and they obviously were not happy. Not happy at all.

"Hey, thanks for telling us to buy Tech-Foots," one guy said, clearly meaning the exact opposite.

"Really awesome shoes," a girl drawled sarcastically.

"We want our money back," another girl demanded.

The kids around her nodded in agreement.

Carly panicked. What could she do? "Well, we didn't sell you the shoes . . ." Carly stammered.

"Fine. Then we're just going to stop watching *iCarly*," another guy said.

The crowd around him turned their backs on Carly and her friends, and stormed off, squeaking with every step.

The *iCarly* team exchanged concerned looks. How many of their fans had gone out and bought Tech-Foots after watching Carly and Sam say how great they were? Every single one of those kids would be as angry with them as their classmates were. Would they lose their entire audience all because of Daka and their lame sneakers? No amount of money was worth that.

Carly glared down at the shoes in her hand. "These Tech-Foots are terrible," she shouted. She threw them into a nearby trash can.

Zaaaaap!

Sparks burst into the air, followed by smoke. Carly's shoes had exploded!

Sam and Freddie didn't take their eyes off of the smoking trashcan. What if the shoes exploded again? Slowly and carefully, they took off their own Tech-Foots and tiptoed away in their socks.

After school, Carly, Sam, and Freddie sat around Carly's kitchen table staring at a Tech-Foot sneaker. They were totally bummed. Everyone in school who had bought the shoes after watching *iCarly* was mad at them. How much longer would it be before they lost their entire audience? Their only consolation was that Sonya was baking something to make them feel better.

Carly glared at the sneaker through narrowed eyes. She grabbed a banana from the fruit bowl on the table and pounded the sneaker with it.

"This is bad," Freddie said.

"It's not that bad," Sam said, trying to calm everyone down.

Was Sam serious? How could this not be bad? Carly turned to her. "Thousands of people are wearing the worst shoe in history because we told them how great they are."

Sam thought about it for a second. "This is bad," she agreed.

They were distracted from their own problem when Spencer came through the front door carrying his homemade bicycle. Only it wasn't exactly a bicycle anymore. It was more like a mangled mess of old bicycle parts. He leaned it up against the kitchen counter with a frustrated grunt. "I need some milk," he said, heading straight to the refrigerator.

"What happened to your homemade bike?" Carly asked.

"I chained it up by the curb for a few minutes, and one of those street-sweeper truck things came by and sucked it right in." Spencer drank a small glass of milk to calm himself down and then poured another.

"Well, maybe you should just start riding the bus again," Carly told him.

"Not happening," Spencer said. "I'll just get around the old-fashioned way."

"You're going to walk everywhere?" Sam asked.

"Nope. I'm going to blade," Spencer said, heading off to find his in-line skates.

Blade? Somehow the idea of Spencer on skates didn't make anyone believe he would do better than he had on a bike.

Even so, at least he had a plan. Sam watched him go and then picked up the Tech-Foot on the table. "So what are we going to do about these Jank-Foots?" she asked.

"We better do something unless we want *iCarly* to keep losing viewers," Freddie told them.

Sonya walked over with a plate full of

fresh-baked muffins. "Blubbery muffins?" she asked.

"What?" Freddie asked. He didn't exactly want to eat muffins made of blubber. He was pretty sure he was allergic to whale.

"Blubbery?" Sonya said again.

Carly examined a muffin. "Blueberry," she said, but didn't reach for one.

"Sorry, Sonya, we're too upset to eat," Sam told her.

With a sad expression, Sonya left the muffins on the table and headed back toward the stove. The warm fresh muffin smell drifted across the table. After a couple of seconds, Carly, Sam, and Freddie decided they could eat after all.

Carly chewed thoughtfully. "How about this?" she asked. "We go talk to the guys at Daka, tell them everything that's wrong with the Tech-Foots, and maybe they'll fix them."

"I think that's smart," Freddie said.

Carly turned to her best friend for her opinion. "Sam?"

Sam didn't answer. She realized Carly and Freddie were staring at her, waiting for her to say

something. "Oh, sorry, I was lost in this muffin," she admitted.

They were interrupted when Spencer skated into the living room, grabbed onto the couch, almost hit the kitchen counter, and spun out of control when he passed Sonya. He wore a helmet, elbow pads, and kneepads, and it was obvious that he needed all the safety equipment known to man.

"Woo hoo hoo!" he shouted, grabbing a muffin. "If you need me, I'll be at the gym," he said. Then he banged into his mangled bike, tripped over the coffee table, and crashed into the door.

Spencer managed to get to the open door. He gave Carly and her friends the peace sign as he skated out. His next problem came when he tried to close the door behind him. He slammed the door into the back of his skate and sent himself flying down the hall.

Sam and Freddie cracked up.

Spencer ignored them. He carefully got to his knees and then to his feet. "Can you get the door?" he yelled over his shoulder.

The next thing Carly heard was Spencer's scream as he smashed into the elevator.

Later, Carly made a call, and the *iCarly* team headed back to Daka for another meeting. The executives were already gathered around the conference table when they arrived.

"Hey, hey, it's the *iCarly* team," Mr. Horvath said, standing to greet them. "How are you guys doing?"

"Not so great," Carly told him. "We need to talk to you about the Tech-Foots."

"They have a ton of problems," Freddie added.

There were concerned murmurs around the table.

Mr. Horvath sat down again. "Problems? Such as?" he asked.

"Well first, they squeak really badly," Sam told him.

"And the Wi-Fi crashed my computer," Freddie said.

Sam continued with the list of problems. "Carly got shocked when she stepped in a puddle."

"And then they practically fell apart," Freddie said.

But that wasn't the worst. Carly had saved the worst for last. "And when I threw them away, they exploded."

Mr. Horvath shrugged his shoulders and chuckled nervously. "Well, you know, when you put out a new shoe, they always have a few minor problems."

Sam could *not* believe Mr. Horvath was shrugging off an explosion. "Minor?" she asked.

Freddie was just as mad. "What would be a major problem?"

"If they came to life in the middle of the night and ate your family?" Carly asked sarcastically.

Mr. Horvath chuckled again. "Oh, I live alone," he said.

Carly exchanged looks with Sam and Freddie. It was time to demand that Daka did its job and fixed the Tech-Foot.

Carly took a deep breath and looked Mr. Horvath right in the eye. "Look, either you make the shoes work like they're supposed to . . ."

". . . or we're never going to talk about them on *iCarly* again," Sam finished.

Freddie mustered up every bit of toughness he had — there wasn't much, but he did his best. "Yeah!" he said with snarl.

Mr. Horvath knew how to get tough himself. "Look," he said seriously. He got to his feet and towered over the *iCarly* team. "You signed a deal with Daka shoes, and you took our money. So, you're going to keep talking up our Tech-Foots on *iCarly*, or you're going to be in big legal trouble."

"We're not scared of you," Freddie said.

"Yeah, my uncle happens to be a lawyer," Sam added.

Carly turned to her, confused. "I thought he got arrested."

"Shhhhhh!" Sam said, trying to get her to be quiet.

They had reached a standoff. The president of Daka wouldn't back down. Neither would Carly, Sam, and Freddie. In the end, the *iCarly* team ended the staring match and left the conference room. It seemed like there was nothing they could do.

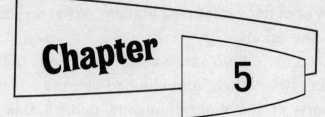
Back at home, Carly and Sam were slumped on the couch while Freddie read the *iCarly* message boards. It seemed like every single viewer who had bought Tech-Foots had posted an angry message.

"Ah, here's another one," he said, reading. "'Why don't you come over to my house so I can put on my new Tech-Foots, and jump up and down on your faces?'"

"This is awful!" Carly moaned.

"I know!" Sam agreed. "Half our audience is mad at us and we're completely out of blubbery muffins."

"Look, on *iCarly* tonight, you guys have to tell everyone that Tech-Foots bite," Freddie said seriously.

"Uh, no thanks," Sam said. "I don't want to get sued for everything I have."

Carly shot her a confused glance. "What do you have?" she asked.

"Oh, yeah," Sam answered, realizing that she didn't have much. And she had already spent her share of the eight thousand dollars Daka paid them the week before. She was about to tell her friends that Daka could go ahead and sue her when Spencer limped in the front door with his in-line skates slung over his shoulder.

"Spencer!" Carly yelled, running over to him and taking his arm. "What happened?"

Sam took his other arm and together the girls helped Spencer limp over to the couch.

"One minute, I'm blading down Hill Street feeling good, on top of the world," Spencer said with a painful groan. "Next thing I know — BAM! — I got a face full of Dumpster."

Spencer threw his skates to the floor. "Well that's it," he announced. "From now on, Spencer's walking." He dropped on to the sofa with a whimper of pain.

"*Awwww,*" Carly said, petting his arm.

Sam watched him for a moment, and then

turned to Carly. "Hey, didn't Spencer go to law school for, like, twenty minutes?" she asked.

"Three days, thank you," Spencer told her.

"Well, do you think you could help us get out of a contract?" Freddie asked.

"What, the Tech-Foot one?" he asked.

"Yeah," Carly said.

"Well, I'd have to read it," Spencer said. "But if there's one thing I learned during my seventy-two hours of law school, it's that every contract has a loophole."

"So, you'll help us?" Freddie asked.

"Sure, but not right now, okay? I just had to walk eight miles to get home, and I'm tired and sad." Spencer flopped over on his side, with his head on a pillow.

"Awwww," Carly said again, rubbing his arm.

Sam leaned over him. "You want a nice bowl of hot soup?" she asked tenderly.

"Yes, please," Spencer said in a little boy voice.

Sam straightened up and screamed. "Sonya!"

Sonya came running. The next thing they knew, she was in the kitchen, cooking up a storm. Sam

was going to miss that when Spencer worked his magic on their contract. There was no way she could afford Sonya on her regular allowance.

A few hours later, Carly, Sam, and Freddie were getting ready for *iCarly*. Spencer had helped them come up with a plan that would honor their Daka contract and clue their fans in to the truth about Tech-Foots at the same time. Carly thought it was brilliant and creative, just like her brother.

Freddie worked his control panel and then picked up his camera.

"In five, four, three, two . . ." he pointed at the girls. The red light on his camera blinked on and they were streaming live on the web.

"Heeeeyyyyyy!!!" Carly and Sam said into the camera.

"Okay, this is *iCarly* . . ." Sam said.

". . . and before we do anything else tonight . . ." Carly said.

". . . we want to talk to you guys some more about the *incredible* new Tech-Foot shoes we told you about last week," Sam finished.

"We're going to show you all the reasons why Tech-Foots are so *unique*," Carly said.

"Hey, Carly?" Sam asked.

"Yes, Sam?" Carly answered.

"Do your feet ever get hot and sweaty?" Sam asked.

"Only always!" Carly told her.

Sam picked up a Tech-Foot and looked into the camera. Freddie panned back so that their viewers could see that she was standing behind a table with a bowl full of water on it. "Well, that's not a problem with Tech-Foots," she said.

"Don't I know it!" Carly agreed.

"Because all you have to do is get them a little wet . . ." Sam dipped the toe of the shoe into the bowl of water to demonstrate.

"Like when it rains," Carly added.

Sam pulled the shoe out of the water and then stuck her hand in it. ". . . and then you can just shove your toes through the front like this." Sam's fingers went right through the toe of the shoe, creating a big hole.

Carly gave the camera a big, fake smile. "How *wonderful*!"

She and Sam nodded enthusiastically into the camera.

At Daka headquarters, the executives had gathered in the conference room to watch *iCarly* live on their plasma screen TV.

They watched in stunned horror as Carly and Sam showed their audience just how flimsy the shoe really was. And the demonstration was about to get worse — much worse.

"And now, our technical producer, Freddie, will show you another cool thing about the Tech-Foot," Carly said into the camera.

The executives watched Freddie carry his laptop over to the table with the shoes. "Okay, if your computer's hard drive is cluttered with a bunch of files, music, and precious pictures of family and friends," Freddie said. "The Tech-Foot does an amazing thing with Wi-Fi technology."

Freddie pushed a button on the shoe and then clicked a few keys on his laptop. "See, you just sync the pedometer up to your computer, and . . ." Freddie held up his laptop to the camera with a big, fake smile. The screen had gone blank. All his data had disappeared. "It wipes out your entire hard drive!"

"Isn't that great?" Sam asked, nodding at the camera.

Mr. Horvath jumped to his feet, totally outraged. "We're going over there," he yelled.

His staff did exactly what he did.

"Over there," someone said.

"Yes, we should go there," another guy agreed.

"Going," Braxley added.

They practically tripped over one another, trying to be the first one through the door to impress the boss.

The *iCarly* team didn't know that the entire Daka executive committee was about to descend on them. Carly and Sam were still going over the *unique qualities* of the Tech-Foot.

"And wait until you see this!" Sam said into the camera.

"For those cold winter days . . ." Carly said.

49

". . . every Tech-Foot comes with a built-in toe warmer!" Sam finished, pretending to be excited.

"And if you turn the toe warmer on high . . ." Carly said.

". . . like this," Sam added, demonstrating. The shoe's toe turned from blue to red, indicating that it was on.

"Then bang it on the table," Carly instructed.

Sam pounded the shoe on the table three times and then dropped it.

She and Carly stepped back as sparks began to shoot out of the Tech-Foot. One second later, it burst into flames.

Freddie laughed as he captured it all on camera.

"It magically catches on fire!" Sam said.

The girls plastered huge smiles on their faces and pretended that a burning shoe was a selling point. But they knew the truth, and they knew the *iCarly* audience was smart enough to catch on to what they were doing.

"Isn't that handy?" Carly asked.

"That'll keep your piggies warm," Sam added.

"And not only that," Carly said into the camera.

That was Sonya's cue. She scurried into the studio, and handed Carly and Sam two long pieces of wire with hot dogs attached to the ends. The girls held the hot dogs over the flaming shoe.

"It's also perfect for . . ." Sam said.

". . . roasting weenies!" Carly and Sam said together.

"So go out right now and buy yourself a pair of Tech-Foots," Sam urged their audience.

"Because this is one hot shoe!" Carly said.

The girls were still roasting their hot dogs over the flaming shoe when Freddie brought the show to a close.

The next thing they knew, Mr. Horvath and his executive committee were pounding on the apartment door and demanding to speak to them.

51

Chapter 6

Mr. Horvath stood in Carly's living room glaring at the *iCarly* team. His executives stood behind him, imitating his angry stare.

"You were warned," Mr. Horvath said furiously. "I warned you! Did I warn them?"

His executives all murmured their agreement. "Oh, yes," one said.

"You did," said another.

Braxley chimed in, focusing his anger on Sam, the sandwich stealer. "You did."

"Not only did you violate your contract by saying bad things about the shoe, you besmirched the name of the Tech-Foot by criticizing it!" Mr. Horvath ranted.

Carly and her friends exchanged glances. This guy was even angrier than they expected.

"You think I won't take legal action against you? You think I'm above suing children?" Mr. Horvath

continued. "Well I'm not! So I hope you have a good lawyer."

Carly eyed him confidently. "Oh, we do," she said.

Spencer ran down the stairs from the studio wearing his only suit and carrying a briefcase. "Gentlemen," he said. "I'm their lawyer."

One thing Spencer knew for sure about lawyers was that they wore ties. He pointed to the bright red one around his neck. "And this is my necktie." But Spencer's necktie was also a statement. He squeezed a button at the end of the tie, and the subtle plaid pattern lit up and started to flash.

"Cool tie," Freddie told him.

"Yeah, where'd you get that?" Sam asked. It reminded her of the crazy light up socks Spencer sometimes wore — socks he got from a guy named Socko!

"Socko's brother Tyler," Spencer said.

Sam nodded. She should have known.

Spencer turned back to Mr. Horvath. "Now, I understand that you're upset with my clients."

"They're in violation of a signed contract," Mr. Horvath snapped.

His executives stood behind him nodding.

Spencer opened his briefcase and pulled out the contract. "This contract says only that the members of *iCarly* must comment about your shoe, the Tech-Foot, in a positive way," Spencer said, reading. He turned his back on the Daka team and started to walk away.

"Which they didn't," Mr. Horvath announced.

Spencer whipped around. "Wrong, sir!" he said. "I've reviewed the Webcast in question, and they said only positive things about the Tech-Foot." Spencer walked over to the computer in the kitchen and turned it on. "Exhibit A!"

He reran clips from the Web show. The whole room watched Sam holding the shoe she had dunked into a bowl of water.

"And then you can just shove your toes through the front to cool them off!" Sam had said on the Webcast. "Like this!"

Mr. Horvath got furious all over again when he watched Sam stick her fingers through the toe of the shoe, showing the *iCarly* audience just how flimsy the shoe really was.

"How wonderful!" Carly had said on the air.

Spencer paused the show. "Exhibit B!" he said, clicking the mouse.

He brought up the clip of Freddie showing their viewers how Tech-Foots could wipe out a computer's hard drive.

On the show, Carly and Sam stood next to him with huge, fake smiles. "Like a magic eraser!" Carly had said.

"Isn't that great!" Sam added.

Mr. Horvath was so mad he was sputtering, but Spencer wasn't finished. He had one more clip ready.

"Exhibit C," he said, clicking the mouse again.

This time, he showed Daka the clip of Carly and Sam standing behind the Tech-Foot — the Tech-Foot on fire that is.

"It's also perfect for . . ." Sam said on the clip.

". . . roasting weenies," she and Carly said together.

Spencer stopped the playback, and then turned

to Mr. Horvath and the rest of the Daka executives. "How wonderful," he quoted. "Isn't that great. Roasting weenies." Spencer walked toward Mr. Horvath, holding the contract. "Those sound like very positive comments to me. Wouldn't you agree? Because I think a judge would. Certainly one who enjoys weenies."

Mr. Horvath snatched the contract out of Spencer's hands and looked it over.

Carly walked up to him. "And we're going to keep talking about the Tech-Foot in a *positive* way," Carly threatened, putting air quotes around the word "positive."

Sam stepped up next to her. "Just like we did tonight," she said.

"To over three hundred thousand *iCarly* fans every week," Freddie added.

Mr. Horvath turned around and whispered to his executives. They formed a tight circle around him so that they wouldn't be over heard by the *iCarly* team.

Carly motioned to Sam, Freddie, and Spencer into a huddle across the room.

"Why are we huddling?" Sam asked in a whisper.

"I don't know, they're doing it," Carly answered.

Mr. Horvath straightened up and turned around. "All right," he said.

Carly and her friends broke their huddle.

"If you'll stop talking about the Tech-Foot on *iCarly* — completely," Mr. Horvath continued. "We're prepared to buy you out of your contract."

"For how much?" Sam demanded.

"Ten thousand," Mr. Horvath said.

"Twenty thousand," Freddie answered.

Mr. Horvath was willing to negotiate. "Fifteen thousand," he countered.

Sam wanted more. "Thirty thousand!" she yelled.

"What?" Mr. Horvath shouted. They couldn't raise their asking price in mid-negotiation.

But they could and they did. Plus they wanted something more — something for the *iCarly* fans who had gone out and bought shoes just because Carly and Sam said they were cool. "And, you have to give full refunds to every *iCarly* viewer who bought Jank-Foots," Carly said.

"Tech-Foots," Freddie corrected.

"I know what I said," Carly told him.

"And what if I say no?" Mr. Horvath asked.

"Then we sue you," Spencer told him.

Mr. Horvath knew he had been beaten. A lawsuit would only draw attention to the mess Daka had made in creating a shoe that squeaked, fell apart, destroyed computers, and caught fire. He didn't want to, but he was forced to agree to the *iCarly* team's terms. "All right!" he said. "Braxley, write her a check for thirty thousand dollars."

"Nuh-uh. Cash," Carly said.

Mr. Horvath sighed and pulled out his wallet, signaling his team to do the same. They began dropping cash onto the coffee table while Carly, Sam, and Freddie watched. Spencer stood back with his arms folded.

Sonya walked in from the kitchen at that moment with a plate full of freshly baked muffins. "Blubbery muffins?"

Carly, Sam, and Freddie all reached for one. So

did Braxley. He was about to take a bite when Mr. Horvath slapped it out of his hand.

Braxley shook his head. "I'm clueless. . . ." he admitted.

"Keep it coming," Sam said.

Freddie smiled. "This is awesome."

Carly had thought that getting the money when they signed the contract was great, but this was even better. "This is fun. This is a fun time," she laughed.

A few days later, Carly led Spencer out of their apartment building and into the parking lot. She had tied a blue bandanna around his eyes so that he wouldn't see his surprise until exactly the right moment.

"Where are we going?" Spencer asked.

Carly shook her head. That was only about the tenth time he had asked her that question in the five minutes it took them to get downstairs. "Can you try not to talk so much?" she said.

"Just give me a hint," Spencer begged.

59

"Oh, look who keeps saying words," Carly teased.

"Well, why can't you tell me why I have to wear this blind —"

Carly cut him off. They had reached their surprise destination. "Hey! Just be quiet and take off your blindfold."

Spencer did as he was told. His jaw dropped when he saw his surprise. He was standing in front of a motorcycle with a big blue bow on it.

Carly giggled and handed him a set of keys.

"Wha — What is this?" he asked, totally blown away.

"A motorcycle," Carly said happily. "I bought it for you so you don't have to ride buses, or junky bikes, or Rollerblade into Dumpsters."

Spencer couldn't believe it. "You spent your Tech-Foot money on me?"

Carly knew she wouldn't have had that money if it wasn't for Spencer. He's the one who had gotten them out of that bad contract. "I got it because of you," she said.

Spencer looked from his surprise to Carly, still not quite believing that the motorcycle was his.

"Youuuuu," he said, too overwhelmed to come up with the right words to tell his sister just how grateful he was.

"Youuuuu," Carly said right back.

Spencer pulled Carly into a huge bear hug and then grabbed one of the two helmets on the bike. "Stick this on your head and get on!" he said.

"Okay," Carly said with a laugh.

Spencer put his helmet on and jumped on the motorcycle.

Carly climbed on behind him and put her hands on his shoulders. "Where are we going?" she asked.

"Canada," Spencer announced.

Carly laughed again. "See, you love their bacon," she joked.

"I do!"

"Even if it is just ham!"

Spencer started the engine. "It's good ham!"

"All ham's good ham!" Carly told him.

"Touché!"

Carly was still laughing when they zoomed out of the parking lot.

iCarly
Saves
Television

Chapter 1

Freddie picked up his camera and focused it on Carly and Sam. It was just about time for this week's *iCarly* Webcast to begin. "In five, four, three, two . . ." he said, and pointed to the girls.

On one, the red light on the camera blinked on. *iCarly* was streaming live on the Internet.

Carly smiled into the camera. "Hey, it's me, Carly!" she said.

"On the other hand, I'm Sam!" Sam said into the camera.

Carly started a sentence. "And this is *iCarly* . . ."

And Sam finished it. ". . . voted the number one Web show in the world!"

Carly turned to her best friend. "By who?" she asked.

Sam grinned. "Me!"

Carly laughed and turned back to the camera. "Then it's official!"

The girls threw confetti into the air, grabbed a couple of noisemakers, and blew them at the camera. Being the number one Web show in the world was something to celebrate, even if Sam was the only one who voted.

Across town, a girl named Morgan was watching Carly and Sam. She sat giggling in front of a laptop computer in her father's office. He happened to work at Seattle's TVS television studio, but Morgan wasn't interested in what was on TV. *iCarly* was much funnier.

Her father, Brad Fesser, came into the office. He stopped short when he saw Morgan glued to a Webcast instead of a television show.

"Morgan," he said.

"Oh, hey, Daddy," Morgan said.

"What are you doing?" Mr. Fesser asked.

"Watching *iCarly* online," Morgan told him.

Mr. Fesser rubbed his forehead and tried to stay calm. He sat down across from his daughter.

"Sweetie, I told you. If Daddy doesn't come up with some TV shows that people your age like, Daddy's going to get fired and have *noooo* more money," he said. "And then you'll starve."

Morgan's eyes got wide. Starve? As in have no food?

Mr. Fesser led Morgan over to a flat screen TV on his office wall. "So, while I go see my boss, I want you to watch this new show we're making. It's really funny."

"Okay," Morgan said with a sigh. She knew that whatever her father and TVS had made wouldn't be nearly as funny as *iCarly*. It never was.

Mr. Fesser hit a button on the remote and the new TV show appeared on the screen. He made sure Morgan was watching, and then left the office in search of his boss.

In the TV show, a girl in a fancy, pink dress was talking to her dad in their living room.

"But, Michelle," the TV dad said. "Why would you accept two dates to the prom, but not tell either boy about the other?"

"Because, Dad! Luke is so sweet. But Brandon is so cute!" the girl playing Michelle said.

"Ahh, noodles!" the TV dad yelled, hitting his palm against his forehead.

The people on the laugh track of the show laughed way too hard. The show wasn't funny. Not funny at all.

"Lame," Morgan said, shaking her head. She made sure her father wasn't in the room, and then Morgan used the remote to turn off the TV. Then she turned up the volume on the laptop to catch the rest of *iCarly*.

"And now . . ." Carly was saying. She pulled on a pair of protective goggles.

Sam lifted a watermelon and set it down on a table in front of Carly. "We're going to see what happens when you take an ordinary water-melon . . ." Sam explained.

". . . and pump it full of pressurized air!" Carly finished.

"Yo! Yo! Pump up da fruit!" Sam rapped.

Morgan watched Sam punch a hole in the watermelon with an air nozzle. A hose connected the nozzle to a pressurized air machine. Carly and Sam ran a safe distance away and pressed a button on the machine.

Freddie focused his camera on the water-melon. Morgan could see it getting bigger and bigger as the *iCarly* team pumped it full of air.

"It's gonna blow!" Sam yelled.

"Come on! Come on," Carly chanted.

The watermelon's skin stretched tighter and tighter. It couldn't take any more air. Suddenly, it exploded, splattering wet, pink watermelon goo all over the *iCarly* studio.

Morgan burst out laughing. It was *hilarious*! She was laughing so hard that she didn't hear her father come back.

Mr. Fesser quietly opened the door to his office. His boss, Nancy Ayres, was right behind him. A look of relief came over his face when he heard Morgan laughing.

"You see, she's right there," Mr. Fesser said. Morgan's laughter was proof that his new show would be a hit. Then he realized that Morgan wasn't watching television. She was watching the Webcast again. "Morgan, what are you doing?" he asked, totally exasperated.

Morgan was still laughing. "Watching *iCarly*."

"What is *iCarly*?" Ms. Ayres asked.

"It's a Web show," Morgan told her, barely taking her eyes off the computer screen.

"I thought I told you to watch our new show," Mr. Fesser said.

"It's lame, Daddy," Morgan admitted.

Ms. Ayres crossed her arms with a frown. She turned to Morgan's dad and imitated Morgan. "It's lame," she repeated.

Morgan stopped paying attention to them. She was too busy looking at the computer screen to see what crazy stunt Carly, Sam, and Freddie would come up with next.

Sam held the air hose up and waved it at the camera. "Now we'll see what happens if we pump air into Freddie's pants!" she announced.

"Whoa, whoa, wait a second," Freddie said. He was trying to keep the camera focused on the girls and avoid Sam at the same time. It wasn't easy.

"Yeah! Pump up da pants," Carly chanted.

The camera wobbled all over the place while Freddie tried to stay out of Sam's reach and keep the show running at the same time. Morgan couldn't see Freddie, but she could hear him.

"These are brand-new pants! Seriously, guys," he said.

Sam kept coming at him. Freddie found himself backed up against the wall. There was no escape.

"Oh, Sam, come on, not my pants," Freddie groaned.

"*Shh*, it'll be fun," Sam told him.

Morgan guessed that Sam was successful. She was running back to Carly behind the pressurized air machine.

Freddie couldn't keep the show going and get the air hose out of his pants at the same time. "Okay, would one of you help me pull this nozzle out?" he asked.

Morgan cracked up again. She watched Carly and Sam stay right where they were, ignoring Freddie's cries for help.

Ms. Ayres wasn't laughing. She glared at Morgan's dad. "If you want to create something good, then why don't you make a show like that one on the Internet?" she asked. "You know, the one that's making your daughter laugh?"

Mr. Fesser swallowed hard. He knew he was in

trouble — big trouble. If he didn't come up with a TV show as funny as *iCarly*, he might lose his job. "That's an excellent idea," he stammered.

But Ms. Ayres didn't hear him. She had already left the office.

Morgan was still laughing at Freddie's predicament. She loved it when Sam tortured him!

"No, no! That's too much air!" Freddie yelled. "My pants can't take it!"

Carly and Sam were cracking up too.

"Carly! Sam!" Freddie pleaded.

Then Morgan heard a loud pop. Thousands of threads of khaki material floated on the computer screen and in the *iCarly* studio. Freddie's pants had exploded.

Mr. Fesser leaned on the back of his daughter's chair. Even he started to laugh. Maybe Morgan and his boss were right, he thought. Maybe he needed a TV show exactly like *iCarly*.

Maybe what he needed was *iCarly* itself.

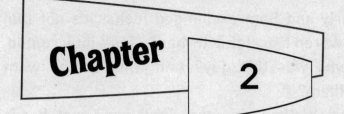

Carly, Sam, and Freddie were in biology class the next morning listening to Mrs. Walker drone on and on as usual. She seemed to believe that what she was talking about was actually interesting. It wasn't.

"So, the hierarchy of the identification system goes, Kingdom, Phylum, Class, Order, Family, Genus —" she pointed at the words on the whiteboard while the students all took notes.

Mr. Fesser rushed into the room, interrupting the lesson. "Hi," he said to the teacher, taking off his sunglasses and looking around the room.

"Yes, can I help you?" the teacher asked.

"I've come for Carly Shay and her friends, Sam and Freddie," Mr. Fesser announced. He spotted Carly and Sam sharing a lab table and gave them a nod.

Carly and Sam exchanged looks. It's not that they weren't grateful to have class interrupted, but who was this guy? And what did he want with them?

Mrs. Walker objected. "You can't just barge into my classroom and demand to take children away without proper —"

Mr. Fesser cut her off. "I run a television network," he said, self-importantly. Obviously, he was used to people being impressed when he said he worked in television. It made them pay attention, and often they did whatever he wanted.

It worked this time, too. Mrs. Walker was suddenly willing to let him take her students away. "Oh. Help yourself," she told him.

Mr. Fesser grabbed the teacher's stool and put it in front of the lab table Carly and Sam shared. Freddie was at the table right behind them. Mr. Fesser leaned toward them with an excited smile.

"Hello," Carly said awkwardly.

"I'm the head of development for TVS," Mr. Fesser explained. "We want to turn *iCarly* into a hit TV show. Will you come with me?"

Carly turned to Sam and Freddie. They were

both smiling and nodding. A hit TV show? There was no question about it. Their answer was a big yes!

"Okay," Carly agreed. "But I should probably call my brother, Spencer. He's the adult that's responsible —"

Carly stopped talking when Spencer ran into the room. His arms were full of fruit and soft drink bottles. "Hey! They picked me up on the way here! In a limo!" he said excitedly. "It's full of fancy sodas and fruits I've never even heard of!" He turned to Mrs. Walker and showed her an orange colored fruit. "This is a guava," he said.

Spencer turned back to Carly and her friends. "Well, c'mon!" he yelled, racing back to the limo.

The *iCarly* team grabbed their books and their backpacks, and followed Spencer down the hall. *iCarly* was going to a TV studio — in a limo!

After a tour of the TVS studio, Carly, Sam, Freddie, and Spencer hung out in Mr. Fesser's office, waiting to hear what he had to say about a TV show based on *iCarly*.

"Okay, everyone, please sit," Mr. Fesser said, rushing in. "Take a seat."

Spencer was already sitting. His lap was full of fancy fruits and foreign soft drinks. He hadn't stopped gushing about all the new flavors he had yet to experience.

Mr. Fesser started to close the door behind him, but Freddie's mother got there just in time to push her way into the office.

"Excuse me. I'm Freddie's mother," she said.

Mr. Fesser opened the door again. "Yes, please come in, Mrs. Benson."

"Oh, I will," she said. Her tone was clear. TV executives didn't scare her. She was going to watch over her son no matter what.

Mr. Fesser clapped his hands together and got to the point. "Now, did you kids like riding in that limousine?" he asked.

"Oh, yeah," Carly said.

"Awesome!" Sam added.

Freddie could only add, "Loved it!"

Spencer's mouth was too full of some kind of new, exotic fruit to answer. He could only nod.

"Well, if you agree to do *iCarly* as a regular show here at TVS, you guys can use that limo whenever you want," Mr. Fesser told them.

Spencer was still completely focused on the goodies he had picked up in the limo. He sipped a red soda. "What country is this soda from?" he asked.

"I don't know," Mr. Fesser answered.

Spencer took another sip. "Well, it's sweet like berries," he said.

Mr. Fesser didn't know what to say so he just said, "Thank you."

Freddie was much more concerned about the technical aspects of the show. He wanted to make sure that TVS would be up to his high standards. Plus he couldn't wait to learn about all the new high-tech gear he would get to play with if *iCarly* made the move to TV. "So, what about stuff like cameras, lighting, audio?" he asked.

"We take care of all those things," Mr. Fesser assured him. "We're even going to recreate your little *iCarly* studio, right here at TVS."

"But then how does Freddie fit in to the TV

show?" Carly asked. She couldn't imagine doing *iCarly* without him, but Mr. Fesser had just said that they would take care of all the technical stuff. That was Freddie's job.

"He's going to be *iCarly*'s new supervising producer," Mr. Fesser said.

"Supervising producer," Freddie repeated. He liked the sound of that. It sounded important.

"Is that dangerous?" Mrs. Benson asked. "Does it involve anything sharp or pointy?"

Mr. Fesser shook his head.

Freddie rolled his eyes. "Mom," he said, trying to get her to be quiet. He was a supervising producer. His mother shouldn't be embarrassing him like that.

Freddie might have been worried about the technical quality of the show, but Sam was thinking about what she always thought about — food.

"What about snacks?" she asked. "Don't TV shows always have a big snack table somewhere?"

"Yes, of course," Mr. Fesser assured her.

Sam wasn't sold yet. The type of snack was

important, too. "And would there be ribs?" she asked.

"Do you like ribs?"

Sam nodded. "Very much, yes."

"Then we'll have ribs."

Sam was completely won over. Limo rides and ribs were all she needed to be completely and totally happy. She leaned over and whispered to Carly. "I think this could be good for us."

Mr. Fesser knew he had sold Sam and Freddie on the idea. But Carly hadn't said whether she was in or out yet. "Carly? Are you in?" he asked.

Carly didn't need to think about it. She was no fool. "A TV show, limos, ribs? I'm not clueless," she told Mr. Fesser. "Yeah, I'm in!"

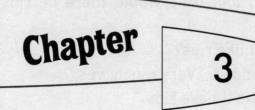

Chapter 3

A week later, Mr. Fesser's assistant led Carly, Sam, and Freddie onto the *iCarly* set at TVS. The team's jaws dropped. The *iCarly* set at the TV studio looked exactly like the third floor of Carly's loft. It had the same window, the same *iCarly* Live sign, even the same wacky light sculptures.

"Whoa!" Sam said.

Carly stopped short, totally amazed. "Oh my gosh!"

"They recreated our whole set," Sam said.

Freddie could only look around, completely astounded by how much it looked like the loft.

Mr. Fesser walked up to them. "Hey, hey! Welcome to television," he said, giving them all fist bumps.

"Hey, the set looks awesome," Carly told him, still surprised that they had gotten every last detail right.

"So cool," Sam added.

"Yeah," Freddie said. Then he spotted some kids on the other side of the stage — where the front end of Spencer's car sculpture usually sat. There was a keyboard, a drum set, and a guitar there, too. It was the only difference from their studio at Carly's loft. "Hey, who are they?" he asked.

"That's your new *iCarly* band," Mr. Fesser said.

Sam couldn't believe it. "We get our own band?"

Mr. Fesser signaled to the keyboard player. "Hey, Harper, come over here!"

Harper jogged over to them.

"What's up, Brad?" he asked.

"I want you to meet the *iCarly* team."

"Oh yeah," Harper said, recognizing them. "I've seen your show online," he told Carly and Sam.

"Yeah?" Carly asked.

"Really?" Sam was just as surprised to learn that a cool musician like Harper watched their Webcast.

"Yeah," Harper said, chuckling. "I loved the one when Sam tied up Freddie and shaved off his eyebrow."

Freddie cringed. It had taken weeks for that eyebrow to grow back. It still didn't match his other eyebrow.

"Thanks," Sam said modestly. "I was just improvising."

"She has anger issues," Carly joked.

"You guys ready for your first rehearsal?" Mr. Fesser asked.

They were all totally psyched.

"Let's rock it," Sam said.

Carly smiled. "Yeah!"

"Let's do it," Freddie said with a nod.

Harper ran over to join his band while Carly and Sam took their usual positions. Only today they weren't standing in front of Freddie and his handheld camera. There were three big TV cameras aimed at them, and a man holding a microphone over their heads.

At least the countdown was familiar. Freddie began. "Okay! Rehearsing in five, four —"

Mr. Fesser cut him off. "Freddie, Freddie, that's the director's job."

"Oh, right," Freddie said, backing up. He was embarrassed to have made such a rookie mistake in front of so many television professionals. "Sorry, everybody. Sorry, band," he said. Then he looked up at the big man holding the script — the one who looked kind of mad. "Sorry, director."

"Here we go," the director said. "In five, four, three, two . . ."

On one, Harper and the band began a rock and roll intro while cool blue and green lights swept the stage. Carly and Sam danced to the music.

"I'm Carly!" Carly said into the camera when the music stopped.

Sam smiled big into the camera. "I'm Sam!"

"And here's our impression of an obnoxious teenage girl arguing with her mother," Carly said.

"Go," Sam told her.

Carly put a hand on her hip and started to whine. "Mo-om, buy me a carrrr!"

Sam glared at her like an irritated mom. "No!" she shouted.

They stayed in character and argued back and forth.

"Mo-om!" Carly whined, rolling her eyes.

"No!" Sam barked.

"Mo-om!"

"No!"

Freddie turned to Mr. Fesser with a grin. This was funny stuff.

Mr. Fesser grinned back.

The girls kept arguing.

"Mo-om!"

"No!"

Finally, Carly bowed, bringing the comedy routine to an end. "Thank you," she said in her own voice.

"Thanks so much," Sam said, bowing alongside her.

Carly looked into the camera. "And now, say hey to *iCarly*'s music dude . . ."

"Harper!" she and Sam said together, pointing to Harper and the *iCarly* band.

There was applause and cheers in the studio.

"Thanks, Carly. Sam," Harper said. "I actually wrote a little song about you guys. It goes . . ." He started to play the keyboard and sing. "Carleeee! Oh, Saaaaam. Yeeeeaaahhhh!"

"Cool song," Sam said.

"What do you call it?" Carly asked.

"I call it 'Carly, Sam, Yeah,'" Harper said with a confused expression. What else would he call it? Then he turned to his band. "Punch it!" he said with a laugh.

Freddie was watching on a monitor, alongside Mr. Fesser.

"Going great, huh?" Mr. Fesser asked.

"Yeah," Freddie said. "But, um, I think the show looks a little too bright. Can we bring down the lighting just a bit?"

"Look, it's really not your job to handle the lighting, okay?" Mr. Fesser said.

Not his job? Freddie had done everything on *iCarly* when it was a Webcast. He had already been told that directing wasn't his job. And now he couldn't comment on the lighting? What exactly was his job, Freddie wondered? "But you said I was going to be a producer," he said.

"Yeah, but you've got to work your way up to producing stuff like lights," Mr. Fesser said.

"Okay," Freddie agreed. He was willing to work his way up to the important parts of the job, but

he wanted to contribute something to the show today. "So what can I produce right now?" he asked.

"Why don't you go produce me a toasted bagel with cream cheese?"

Freddie glared at him, but there was nothing he could do. *iCarly* had moved to TV, and Freddie wasn't calling the shots anymore. Mr. Fesser was. The supervising producer trudged off to find a bagel and a toaster.

At home, Spencer was folding laundry in the living room when the doorbell rang. "Coming," he said.

Mrs. Benson was at the door with a plate of food.

"Hey, Mrs. Benson. What's up?"

"By force of habit I made some after school snacks for Freddie," she explained. "But since he's at rehearsal, I thought maybe you'd like to share them with me."

Spencer hesitated. There was a reason why Freddie was always eating at Carly and Spencer's house. His mother's cooking was so healthy that even health nuts found it hard to eat. "I really . . ."

Mrs. Benson interrupted. "Share them with me!" she said with a desperate expression.

"All right," Spencer said, heading back to his laundry.

Mrs. Benson followed him in, explaining her snacks. "These are cucumber cups filled with low-fat yogurt and chopped celery."

Cucumber with low-fat yogurt didn't sound at all appealing to Spencer. "I really don't think I've ever —"

Mrs. Benson didn't give him a chance to say no. She shoved a cucumber cup into Spencer's open mouth, forcing him to chew.

"Interesting flavor," Spencer said, trying not to choke.

"Thank you." Mrs. Benson put the plate down. She sighed and turned away.

Spencer quickly spit the cucumber cup into his hand and flung it into the kitchen.

Mrs. Benson didn't notice. She turned back to Spencer and admitted the real reason for her

visit. She missed Freddie. "You know, it is so lonely in the afternoon without Freddie."

"Yeah, it's pretty quiet around here without Carly, too," Spencer said. "I've been doing laundry to help keep my mind —"

Mrs. Benson was desperate for anything that would keep her mind off the fact that Freddie wasn't at home. "I can help with your laundry," she said eagerly. She reached into the basket and picked up a pair of underpants.

"Oh thanks," Spencer said, trying to stop her. "But seriously, you don't have —"

Mrs. Benson examined the underpants. "Where's your name?" she asked, turning the underpants around and around to see the whole waistband.

"Huh?" Spencer asked.

"You don't have your name sewn into your underpants," Mrs. Benson said.

His name? Did Mrs. Benson think he was going to sleepaway camp or something? Had she forgotten that he was an adult?

"No," Spencer said politely. "No, I'm a grown man."

"A grown man who's going to lose his under-pants," Mrs. Benson countered.

"Well, I —"

"I'll go get my sewing machine," Mrs. Benson said happily. "You finish the cucumber cups."

Spencer tried to tell her he didn't want her after-school snack. "Cucumbers really aren't my —"

But Mrs. Benson was already rushing across the hall, happy to have something to do.

"And you're gone," Spencer said to himself. He realized that he had no choice. He was going to have to eat those cucumber cups, and by the end of the afternoon all of his underpants would have his name sewn into the waistband. Grown man or not. What else was Mrs. Benson going to do to him?

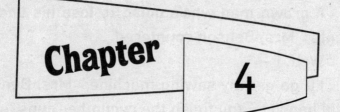

Chapter 4

While Spencer was being forced to entertain Mrs. Benson, Carly and Sam were wrapping up their first television rehearsal.

"Now, before we go," Sam said into the camera.

"We just want to remind you . . ." Carly said.

Sam pointed to a flat screen monitor on the wall. "That's what the Earth looks like from outer space."

A satellite picture of the Earth appeared on the screen. It was surrounded by stars.

"And this is what Earth looks like dressed up as a little girl!" Carly said.

A bell rang, and suddenly the screen showed the Earth wearing a pink party dress. A big pink bow sat on the top of the North Pole.

Sam laughed. "Okay, thanks for watching *iCarly!*"

"Harper, jam us out!" Carly said with a smile.

"Punch it!" Harper said.

He and the band played an upbeat good-bye riff while Carly and Sam danced and waved good-bye to the camera. They had just finished their very first TV rehearsal. It had been a good one too. Carly and Sam thought their show rocked!

The crew clapped and cheered.

"And great rehearsal, everyone!" the director announced. "Take five."

Harper walked over to the girls during their five-minute break. "Hey, nice stuff. You guys are hilarious," he said.

Carly and Sam had barely had time to say thanks before Mr. Fesser walked up behind Harper, clapping. "Incredible. I loved it," he said. He turned to Harper. "Harper, can I talk to the girls alone?"

"Can I drive your new Porsche around the parking lot?" Harper asked.

Mr. Fesser shot him a double take. "How old are you?"

"Fourteen," Harper admitted.

Mr. Fesser thought about it for a minute, and

then handed him the keys. He liked to keep the talent happy when he could. "Drive slow," he warned.

"Yeah, right," Harper said sarcastically.

Carly looked around. If Mr. Fesser was going to talk to them about the show, they needed their supervising producer on hand, and he was nowhere in sight. "Hey, where's Freddie?" she asked.

"He's cleaning out my fish tank," Mr. Fesser said. "So listen, I thought rehearsal went great. Like perfect."

"Cool," Carly said.

"Sweet," Sam added.

Then Mr. Fesser got to the real point. "But I'd like to make some changes."

Changes? Carly didn't understand. He just said he loved the show. "Why change anything?" she asked.

"You just said it was perfect," Sam added.

"It was," Mr. Fesser said. "But we don't feel Harper should talk so much."

Sam was confused. She and Carly had bounced things off of Harper and the band throughout the

show. It kept the show's energy up, and Harper was hilarious. "Why not?" she asked.

Carly was just as puzzled. "He's really cool and funny."

"I know, but we just did some testing, and our research shows that kids love dinosaurs," Mr. Fesser said.

Yeah, Sam thought. *Little kids, not* iCarly*'s regular audience.* She was starting to get a really bad feeling. Did Mr. Fesser think their fans were in preschool? "What are you talking about?" she asked.

Mr. Fesser grinned. "I'm talking about Zeebo."

Carly's stomach sank. She and Sam looked at each other. "Zeebo?" they asked at the same time. They didn't know who or what Zeebo was, but this didn't sound good. Not good at all.

A half an hour later, Carly and Sam were getting ready for their second rehearsal. The director counted them down. "In five, four, three, two . . ."

Carly looked into the camera. She was a lot less excited than she had been for the first rehearsal. "I'm Carly," she said, forcing a smile.

"And I'm Sam," Sam added.

Someone wearing a big blue-and-yellow dinosaur costume hopped in front of the camera. "And I'm Zeebo!" it said, giggling. Zeebo started to dance, and then it swung its hips around, knocking Sam into Carly.

The drummer hit his cymbal.

Carly gave Zeebo a dirty look. She wasn't so thrilled with the band either. She turned to Harper for an explanation.

Harper shrugged. He was following orders. "I've been told not to speak," he said.

Sam and Carly tried to hide their annoyance.

"Okay," Carly said into the camera with a forced smile.

"Welcome to *iCarly*," Sam said through clenched teeth.

Carly was ready to introduce their first segment. "Now today, we're going to —"

Zeebo jumped in front of her. "I'm Zeebo! Whoa!" it said, giggling and dancing. It swung his hip into Sam again, sending her into Carly.

Once again, the drummer hit his cymbal.

94

Sam was getting really annoyed. "You want to quit doing that?" she asked the dinosaur.

"Nope," Zeebo giggled. Then it did it again and this time it shouted, "Kaboom!"

"Hey, could you lower the microphone a little bit?" Sam asked the sound technician.

He lowered the metal pole over Sam's head. The microphone was attached to the end of it, out of Sam's reach.

"A little lower," Sam said, stretching for it. "A little lower." She was finally able to grab onto the mic. "Yeah, thanks."

Sam detached the foam microphone cover from the metal pole and used it to hit Zeebo. If there was one thing Sam couldn't stand, it was being pushed around — especially by a big, fuzzy dinosaur. It was a good thing the dinosaur costume was heavily padded, because Sam knocked Zeebo to the ground and thumped its head with the microphone cover over and over and over. . . .

Harper and the band cracked up. It was the first funny thing on the *iCarly* show since the dinosaur showed up.

Carly looked over at Mr. Fesser to make sure he got the point. "Yeah, kids *loooove* dinosaurs," she said sarcastically.

Sam was still showing Zeebo how much she disliked it.

"Ow! Ow!" Zeebo yelled. "Oh, breaking the face! Breaking the face! Breaking the face of Zeebo!"

Harper and the band started playing music to go with Sam's beating. They didn't like the dinosaur any better than she did.

"Hurting Zeebo!" the dinosaur yelled. "Help Zeebo! Help Zeebo! Get her off!"

The director ran over. "Cut! Cut it! Cut!" he yelled.

Mr. Fesser followed.

Carly tried to pull her friend off the dinosaur. "Sam . . . Sam, c'mon Sam," she said. "I think you've made your point."

Carly was able to pull Sam away from Zeebo, and the dinosaur slowly got to its feet.

The actor playing Zeebo took off the giant, blue head. "I don't have to take this, you know! I did four episodes of *Full House*!" the guy yelled. Then

he threw his Zeebo head at Mr. Fesser and stormed off the set.

"Ethan!" Mr. Fesser called after him. "Look, don't do this."

Ethan didn't listen. They heard a door slam off-stage. Zeebo was gone.

Carly pretended to be sad about it all. "*Awwww.* Personally, I loved Zeebo. But I guess we'll just have to do the show without him."

"Oh, bummer," Sam said sarcastically.

Mr. Fesser didn't get the sarcasm. "Don't worry. Anyone can play Zeebo," he said. He thought for a minute, and then looked over at the band. "Hey, Harper, c'mere."

"What's up?" Harper asked.

Mr. Fesser handed him the dinosaur head. "Put this on," he ordered.

Harper was clearly annoyed, but he reluctantly pulled on the dinosaur head over his own.

"There, you look great," Mr. Fesser said.

"I don't want to play Zeebo!" Harper said.

Mr. Fesser grabbed Harper by the mask. "We have a contract, and you'll play whatever I tell you to play," he said firmly.

"Let go of my snout," Harper said. He stormed off, still wearing the mask.

"How's he going to play keyboards if he's wearing that dumb Zeebo costume?" Carly asked.

"Don't worry about that. We're getting rid of the band completely," Mr. Fesser said.

Carly couldn't believe it. The band was great! It was the only good thing the TV studio had added to the show. "But why?" she asked.

"So we'll have more time for Zeebo," Mr. Fesser said brightly.

Sam glared at him. Zeebo was all right for a little kids show, but he was all wrong for *iCarly*. "Zeebo is a horrible idea," she said.

Mr. Fesser ignored her and checked his watch. "Oh, I'm late for a thing with a guy," he said, hurrying off.

Sam watched him go. "He's ruining *iCarly*," she said sadly.

"Zeebo," Carly said disgustedly. "How long before that nub dresses me up like a dinosaur and starts calling me Carbo?" she asked.

Freddie walked up carrying a bag filled with

98

ice. "Hello," he said. He sounded totally bummed.

"What's that?" Sam asked.

Freddie frowned. "Bag of ice."

"For what?" Carly asked.

"Mr. Fesser told me there's some guy who works here that got all sweaty, and I'm supposed to cool him down," Freddie said. He sounded more than a little sick about the whole idea.

A big guy under the lights called to Freddie. "Over here," he said.

The *iCarly* team looked at the guy and then at Freddie. The guy was a giant sweat ball. It was gross.

When he heard he was going to be a supervising producer, Freddie imagined wheeling and dealing in the world of television. He imagined helping the studio make *iCarly* the top new TV show in the country. He definitely did not imagine sweaty guys and bags of ice. Freddie swallowed hard and trudged over.

Carly and Sam watched him go, totally horrified.

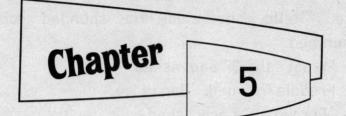

Chapter 5

Back at home Spencer was horrified, too, but for different reasons than Carly, Sam, and Freddie. Mrs. Benson had finished sewing Spencer's name into his underwear and was now supervising every move he made.

When he climbed a ladder to work on his bottle robot, Mrs. Benson stood at the foot of the ladder. Every few seconds she reminded him to be careful, and she insisted on holding his tools.

"Careful, Spencer," Mrs. Benson said, breaking his concentration.

Spencer dropped a bottle and it crashed to the floor, breaking into a million pieces.

"I'm fine," Spencer said. "Just hand me the screwdriver."

"Okay, but caution," Mrs. Benson said, holding it up. "The tip is pointy."

Spencer chuckled. "I've used a screwdriver lots of times, I really don't think —" Spencer expected her to hand the tool to him pointy side down. He reached for it without looking and stabbed himself in the hand. He dropped the screwdriver and yelped.

"I warned you," Mrs. Benson said.

Spencer climbed down the ladder, sucking on his palm to ease the pain.

"Let me see it," Mrs. Benson said.

Spencer resisted. "It's fine," he said. Then he looked at it himself. "Oh my gosh, it's bleeding. We've got a bleeder," he yelled. "My hand is bleeding!"

Mrs. Benson inspected his hand. It was just a small cut, but Spencer was totally overreacting. Even so, she seemed excited to have something motherly to do. "I'll go get my first aid kit," she said, running across the hall.

Spencer was a little woozy from seeing his own blood. "Wait! I don't think I should be left alone," he yelled after her. "There's a hole in my hand."

Mrs. Benson was already across the hall in her own apartment.

"Mrs. Benson?" Spencer called weakly. "Mrs. Benson?"

Mrs. Benson ran back in, carrying a bright red first aid trunk. It was gigantic. "Everything's fine," she told Spencer. "I've got my first aid kit."

Spencer forgot about his hand for a moment. "Wow, that's large."

"Thank you," Mrs. Benson said proudly. She opened the trunk. It was filled with a ridiculous amount of first aid equipment. She quickly selected a spray bottle. "Hold out your hand," she said.

"Is it going to sting?" Spencer asked. "Because I don't want it to —"

Mrs. Benson sprayed his palm.

"*Owww!*" Spencer screamed. Then he realized that the spray didn't hurt at all. In fact, it felt cool and soothing. "Ooo, that's nice."

Mrs. Benson wiped his palm and then put a Band-Aid over the cut. "The bandage," she said. "And you know what's going to make you feel even better?" she asked.

Spencer had spotted a plastic container of lol-lipops in the trunk. "A visit from Doctor Lollipop?" Spencer asked, hoping he was right.

Mrs. Benson pulled one out of the first aid kit. "A visit from Doctor *Sugar-Free* Lollipop," she corrected.

"*Okaaaaay,*" Spencer said. He took the lollipop and forgot all about his pain.

Mrs. Benson was completely happy. She liked nothing better than taking care of people. If Freddie wasn't home to be taken care of, Spencer would have to fill in for him. "Lick slower," she instructed.

At the TV studio the next day, Carly and her friends were hanging out by the food service table. There was a plate piled high with ribs in the center. Sam had already emptied it once, and the studio had brought more.

Sam grabbed a rib and took a bite, getting bar-becue sauce all over her face. "*Mmm.* I hate this TV network, but I love the ribs."

Carly laughed. Sam looked like she was in rib

heaven. That would make a funny bit on *iCarly*, but the network would never go for it. Zeebo's big, blue, fuzzy hands couldn't grasp ribs.

"*Mmmm*, the sauce is so thick and rich," Sam said to Carly. "Look at this." Sam reached out and slapped her rib against Freddie's cheek to demonstrate. The sauce was so thick that the rib stuck to his face. It didn't even slip.

Freddie simply stared at her. This was the least of the humiliations he had suffered at the TV studio.

Sam wiped her mouth with her hand. "That's good barbecue sauce," she pronounced. She pulled the rib off Freddie's cheek and started to eat again.

Freddie glared at Sam and then turned to Carly. "You understand that this is wrong," he said.

Carly was kind of grossed out. "Yes," she agreed.

A girl walked by with a bag over her shoulder. There were tissues sticking out of it, so Freddie grabbed a couple and wiped his face.

Mr. Fesser ran over, excited about his new ideas for the show. "Hey, guys, good news. The network execs watched the tape of yesterday's rehearsal, and they loved it," he said. "They are cuckoo for *iCarly*."

Carly grimaced. She knew what was coming when Mr. Fesser said he loved something. It really meant he wanted to make it different. "But you just want to change —"

"One thing," Mr. Fesser said.

"Shocker," Carly said sarcastically.

"This involves you, Sam," he said.

Sam shot him an irritated look. "If you try to put that dinosaur head on me, I swear —"

"No, nothing like that," Mr. Fesser said, cutting her off. "You're fired."

"What?" Freddie asked.

"You can't fire Sam!" Carly yelled.

"Whoa, wait, whoa," Sam said to her friends. Maybe getting fired wasn't the worst thing that could happen. She turned to Mr. Fesser. "If you fire me, do I still get paid for the whole week?" she asked.

"Yes," Mr. Fesser said.

That's all Sam needed to hear. "Later," she said to her friends. She walked off the set without a second thought. This TV thing had turned out to be a total drag, except for the ribs. She couldn't care less about doing the show if she had to perform with a dinosaur.

"Sam, don't go!" Carly yelled after her. She turned to Mr. Fesser. "I can't do *iCarly* without Sam. She's my co-host," she told him.

"Sorry, but our executives found her pushy and aggressive," he explained.

"She *is* pushy and aggressive!" Freddie agreed. He was too often the brunt of her jokes, but he knew that the *iCarly* fans loved that about Sam.

"That's her thing!" Carly explained.

"Carly, relax. You won't have to do the show alone," Mr. Fesser told her. "We got you a new co-host."

"Who?" Carly asked suspiciously.

"Amber Tate," Mr. Fesser said with a smug expression.

"The movie star?" Freddie asked.

Mr. Fesser nodded. "Yep. She's right over there, getting her makeup done."

Carly and Freddie looked across the studio.

Amber Tate was sitting in a makeup chair, holding a little, white, poofy dog.

"Wow. Can I meet her?" Freddie asked.

"No, but you can meet her dog." Mr. Fesser snapped his fingers, and an assistant took the dog from Amber Tate and carried it over to Freddie.

Freddie's face fell. "Her dog?" he asked.

"Yeah, I need you to give it a bath," Mr. Fesser said.

"Be careful," the assistant warned. "He vomits a lot."

Mr. Fesser patted Freddie on the shoulder. "Have fun," he said lightly, walking away.

Sam was fired. Freddie was an errand boy. And all the fun was being drained out of *iCarly*. This wasn't what they'd signed on for when they agreed to do *iCarly* on TV. Carly stopped Mr. Fesser.

"Okay, look, Brad, nothing against you or Amber Tate or her vomiting dog, but this isn't turning out like I thought it would," she said. "I like doing my show with Freddie behind the camera and Sam standing next to me. So, I think I'll just go home and keep making *iCarly* the way we like it." Carly turned her back to him and started to leave. Freddie was right behind her. They knew they'd find Sam next to the ribs.

"Yeah, sorry, you can't do that. We own the title *iCarly* now," Mr. Fesser said.

Carly whirled around. They owned her name?

"And we own you," he said to her.

Own her?

Carly and Freddie stared at each other and then turned back to Mr. Fesser.

"Aw, c'mon! Get psyched!" he said with a smile. "It's going to be great. Just read the new script," he urged.

Carly took the script from him. "Wait, wait," she said. "Sam and I write our own scripts."

"Not anymore," Mr. Fesser said happily. "We hired professional comedy writers." He turned Carly and Freddie around and pointed to three old guys across the studio.

"Hey, you know where the ribs are?" one of them asked.

"We heard there were ribs," said another.

"Are there ribs?" asked the third.

Mr. Fesser laughed hysterically, as if the three old guys had just written the funniest skit ever.

Carly and Freddie couldn't even pretend to smile. This was going to be the *lamest* show ever!

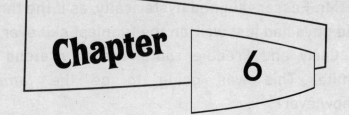

Chapter 6

Later that day, Carly was ready for yet another rehearsal, this one with Amber Tate instead of Sam. Zeebo was still in the show. Harper was being forced to play him.

The director got things started. "*iCarly* rehearsal in five, four, three, two . . ." He pointed at Carly and Amber.

Carly had tried to get psyched, but she was totally bummed. She just couldn't get excited about this new version of *iCarly*. "Hello, people who own televisions. My name is —"

Amber Tate jumped in front of Carly. "I'm Amber Tate," she said spreading her arms wide.

Carly held a hand up and waved to the camera. "Carly," she said weakly.

Harper, playing Zeebo, trudged over. "I'm Zeebo."

"And this is *iCarly*," Carly said into the camera.

Then she looked at the people around her. "Kind of," she added.

Amber seemed to think the show was called *iAmber*, not *iCarly*. She smiled big and took over. "Now, to kick off the show, how about a little song from our friend Zeebo?"

Zeebo danced around half-heartedly and sang a super-lame song about hugging. "H-U-G-G-I-N-G," he sang. "A hug for you is a hug for me."

Carly stared in complete disgust, but Amber danced behind the dinosaur like he was the coolest.

Harper was about halfway through the song when he realized he just couldn't go through with this job. Contract or no contract, it was way too lame. He took off his Zeebo head. "Stop the music. Stop the music," he said. "Hold the track, man!"

The music stopped. Mr. Fesser walked over, clearly annoyed that the rehearsal was being held up. "What's wrong?" he asked.

"This show is jank," Harper told him.

Mr. Fesser turned to Carly for a translation. "Jank?" he asked.

Carly was too mad to be nice to him. "It means bad. Lame. Suckish," Carly told him. "Catching on, Brad?"

"Jank!" Harper said again. He shoved the Zeebo head into Mr. Fesser's hands and walked off the set. "And I crashed your Porsche!" he yelled over this shoulder.

"My Porsche?!" Mr. Fesser yelled. "Aw, Zeebo!"

"Do not call me Zeebo!" Harper said, slamming a door on his way out.

Freddie walked up, holding Amber's dog as far away from his body as his arms could reach.

"Freddie," Carly said, eyeing the stains on her friend's shirt.

"The dog puked on me four times," Freddie told her. He sounded as if he might puke himself.

Amber didn't like the way her precious little pile of fluff was being handled. "Give me him!" she demanded. She buried her face in the dog's fur for a moment, then turned on Freddie. "What'd you do to him?" she asked.

She didn't give Freddie a chance to answer before she thumped him on the forehead.

"*Ow!*" Freddie yelled.

Carly turned on Amber. "Don't thump him!" she said.

Amber held her hand up. "Don't even talk to me," she said.

"Too late, I'm already talking to you," Carly yelled. "And since I am, what is with you chick celebrities carrying around your prissy little dogs? I've had chicken wings with more meat on them than that thing!"

Amber glared at Carly. No one talked to her that way. No one! She was Amber Tate, the movie star! "Well, when you're ready to apologize to me and Biddy-Boo, we'll be in my dressing room," she said, turning on her heel and stomping off with her little dog.

Mr. Fesser came back into the studio carrying a plunger. "Hey, kid," he said, handing it to Freddie. "Go unclog the toilet in my office."

Freddie took the plunger. He stared at it for a second, and then looked at Carly. He had put up with a lot, but plunging toilets was where he drew the line. He was totally fed up. "No," he shouted. "I toasted your bagel, cleaned your fish tank, got yacked on by Amber Tate's rat-dog, and I even rubbed ice all over a sweaty guy's stomach," he yelled. "But I will not plunge your toilet!"

"C'mon, you're my supervising producer," Mr. Fesser coaxed.

"Yeah, well I ain't supervising what you produced in there!" he yelled, pointing in the direction of Mr. Fesser's office. Then he turned to Carly. He knew that she was upset about losing Sam, and he wanted to be there for her, but this was just too much. "I'm sorry, Carly. I quit." He threw the plunger down and walked off the set.

Carly watched him go. "Well, now we've lost Sam, Freddie, and Harper," she said.

"Everything's going to be fine," Mr. Fesser told her.

"Fine?" Carly asked, completely amazed. "This isn't even *iCarly* anymore."

"Oh, c'mon, how can you say —" Mr. Fesser stopped to think for a moment. "You know, you're right. This isn't *iCarly* anymore," he said happily.

Carly recognized that sinister gleam in Mr. Fesser's eye. She had seen it right before he added Zeebo to the show and right before he fired

Sam. He was going to make just one more *little* change.

Three months later, Carly, Sam, and Freddie were on the couch in the loft, waiting to see the first episode of TVS's new show. Spencer ran in with a big bowl of popcorn.

"So this is what TVS did with *iCarly*?" Spencer asked, plopping down between Carly and Sam.

"Uh-huh," Sam said, reaching into the popcorn bowl. "They turned it into a sitcom."

"And they're not even calling it *iCarly* anymore, so we got the name back," Freddie added.

The show was about to start. "*Shhh*, let's watch," Carly said, turning up the volume.

Zeebo and Amber Tate were on the screen.

"But, Michelle, why would you accept two dates to the prom, without telling either boy about the other?" the Zeebo character asked.

"Because, Dad! Luke is so sweet. But Brandon is so cute!" Amber Tate said.

Spencer cringed when a laugh track played much too loudly in the background.

"Aw, noodles!" the Zeebo character said. He swung his hips into Amber, knocking her right out of the frame.

Carly, Sam, Freddie, and Spencer stared at the screen. Then they all used the same word to describe the show: "Lame!"

Carly turned off the TV, relieved that TVS had let her go when they did. Imagine if she had been made to play Zeebo! Limo rides and ribs couldn't make up for that.

That night, the *iCarly* team happily got ready for a live Webcast in their own studio on the loft's third floor.

Freddie rested his camera on his shoulder. "In five, four, three, two . . ." he said.

The light on the camera blinked on.

"Howdy, y'all! I'm Carly!" Carly said into the camera.

"I'm Sam," Sam said.

"And this is *iCarly*!" Carly said with a big smile.

"Back on the Internet," Sam added.

Carly nodded. "Where nobody can tell us what to do."

"Yeah, baby," Freddie said, working the camera.

"And now, Carly will spell the word 'punctuality,'" Sam said.

"While Sam screams like a girl in a horror movie, about to be eaten by a monster," Carly added.

Sam grabbed the sides of her head and screamed at the top of her lungs, while Carly slowly and loudly spelled the long word over Sam's screams. "P-U-N-C-T-U-A-L-I-T-Y."

It was exactly the kind of wacky thing their fans expected, and exactly the kind of thing that Brad Fesser wouldn't understand. He was as lame as the silly sitcom they had just seen on television.

Sam stopped screaming when Carly reached the end of the word. "Nice job, Carls."

"Thank you, Sam."

Freddie laughed from behind the camera.

Sam was ready to introduce the next act. "And now on *iCarly* . . ." she began.

". . . some live music from a new friend of ours who's amazingly talented," Carly finished.

"So let's get him out here . . ." Sam said.

Together, the girls sang his name. "Harper!"

Harper came onto the set with his guitar and gave each of the girls a little hug. He sat on a stool and leaned into the microphone. "This one's for the real *iCarly*," he said.

Harper sang a totally awesome song.

Carly and Sam danced in their seats while Freddie worked his magic with his control panel, switching from a close up of Harper on the stationary camera to a shot of the girls with his handheld.

Everyone was happy. Harper got to sing without wearing a Zeebo costume, Freddie didn't have to clean up after anyone's dog, and Carly and Sam got to be just as wild and wacky as they were meant to be.

iCarly was back!

Read more adventures featuring Carly, Sam, and Freddie!